Campfire Tales:

Lore of the Olympic National Forest

By R.S. Hughes

Campfire Tales:

Lore of the Olympic National Forest

To purchase:
https://tinyurl.com/campfire-tales

For inquiries please contact:
New Horizons Inc.
Newh26441@gmail.com

For my family, with love to Missy and my wonderful grandchildren: Kelson, Makaya, and Charlotte.

Adventure awaits!

Table of Contents:

The Haunting of Highway 101

It was a cold, foggy evening, just about twilight when Jake and Emmy decided to take a road trip on the infamous Highway 101. The two friends were exploring the lesser-known routes of Washington State and wanted to explore landmarks from a popular TV series. As they approached the dense, misty woods surrounding Lake Crescent, a sense of unease settled over them.

"Have you heard about the legend of Highway 101?" Emmy asked with apprehension.

Jake glanced at her with curiosity. "No, what legend?"

Emmy leaned in closer, her eyes wide with a mix of excitement and fear. "They say that somewhere around here, there's a woman who hitchhikes. If you pick her up, you'll never be seen from again."

Jake laughed nervously. "Sounds like something out of a Stephen King novel."

As they continued their drive, the fog grew thicker, and visibility was difficult but not unmanageable.

Suddenly, through the mist, they spotted a figure standing on the side of the road. It was a woman in a white dress, her long dark hair cascading over her face, her dress damp from the moist air.

"Do you see that?" Emmy gasped.

Jake slowed the car to a crawl. "We can't just leave her out here. It's freezing."

Emmy hesitated. "Jake, what if it's her? The woman from the legend?"

Jake shook his head. "It's just a story, Em. Let's see if she needs help."

He pulled over, and the woman approached the car. Her eyes were dark, hollow, and her voice was barely audible. "Can you give me a ride?"

Emmy felt a chill run down her spine. "Where are you headed?"

The woman smiled faintly, a half crooked smile. "Just a bit further down the road. Please, I have to get home."

Against Emmy's better judgment, Jake unlocked the car doors. Without raising an arm the woman opened the backdoor and climbed into the backseat. Emmy wasn't sure what she saw but decided not to mention it. As they drove on, the atmosphere grew tense. The radio crackled with static, and an unnatural coldness filled the car.

"It's cold in here," Jake said, reaching to turn up the heat. "What's your name?" Jake asked, glancing in the rearview mirror.

The woman didn't respond. Instead, she stared out of the window, her expression blank. Emmy's anxiety grew with each passing moment.

Suddenly, the car jolted violently; the engine choked and sputtered before dying completely. While coasting, Jake pulled over and tried to restart it, but it was no use. They were stranded in the middle of nowhere, surrounded by an oppressive fog.

"We should call for help," Emmy suggested, her voice trembling, while reaching for her phone.

Jake nodded and reached for his phone, but they had no signal. "Great, just our luck."

The woman in the backseat began to moan softly, a chilling sound that sent shivers down their spines. "I have to get home," she whispered.

Jake and Emmy turned to her, and before they could react, the woman's form twisted and distorted, her eyes glowing with an otherworldly blood-red light. She lunged at them, screaming, "I HAVE TO GET HOME," her fingers elongated into sharp, spectral claws.

Both Jake and Emmy screamed in terror, panic setting in as they tumbled out of the car. The woman vanished into thin air, leaving behind an icy mist.

Jake and Emmy couldn't see each other or the car through the thick fog. They called to each other, "Jake, where are you?" "Em, I'm here, I can't see you." But as they kept calling to each other, their voices grew further and further apart, only to realize they were completely alone and lost in the dense, haunted fog.

Days later, a state patrol officer found Jake and Emmy's abandoned sedan on the side of Highway 101. There was no trace of the two friends. The only clue was a distorted picture on a dashcam that shows a woman in white on the side of the road. Their disappearance remains a mystery. The legend of the woman in white grew, warning travelers not to pick up hitchhikers on this haunted stretch of road.

The Curse of the Enchanted Pinecone

Deep within the dense, fog-laden woods of the Olympic National Forest, an unsettling transformation was about to begin. It all started with a single pinecone—a seemingly innocuous remnant of the infamous Aokigahara Forest in Japan, also known as the Suicide Forest. During one routine inspection at Port Angeles, the pinecone, filled with ominous seeds, tumbled from a cargo container and landed in the bed of a hunter's pickup truck, unnoticed.

The hunter, unaware of his sinister cargo, drove deep into the forest to set up camp for the night. As he unloaded his gear, the pinecone fell to the forest floor, rolling into the underbrush. The hunter's dog, curious, picked it up and carried it further into the dense woods, eventually dropping it near a cluster of ancient trees. The seeds from the pinecone took root, and an eerie blight began to spread. The trees, once lush and vibrant, now seemed to pulse with a malevolent energy, their twisted branches whispering secrets of despair.

A few years later, the forest was transformed. Hikers and campers who ventured into the area started to experience vivid hallucinations, overwhelming fear, and a crushing sense of hopelessness. The longer you stayed the stronger it felt. One fateful afternoon, a group of friends decided to brave the forest, lured by the thrill of an adventure. Among them were Jenna, Chris, and Alex, all seasoned hikers with a passion for exploration.

"Alright, who's ready for the ultimate adventure?" Chris grinned as he adjusted his backpack.

Jenna rolled her eyes but smiled. "You always say that, Chris. How about we avoid getting lost this time?"

Alex laughed. "Yeah, remember last time we ended up following that 'shortcut' you suggested?"

Chris waved them off playfully. "Details, details. We still had fun, right? This time it'll be different!"

As they started out on their journey, the further they went into the woods, they noticed no birds or the sounds of animals. Just an eerie wind blowing through the trees.

Hours passed as they made their way deeper into the woods, a thick fog enveloped them, and the air grew heavy and cold with an unsettling presence. Jenna shivered. "Guys, do you feel that? Something's not right."

Chris scoffed, trying to mask his own unease. "It's just the fog, Jenna. Let's keep going."

But Alex, the most sensitive of the group, couldn't shake the growing sense of dread. "I don't like this. We should turn back."

Chris reassured everyone, "It's fine. It will clear up soon. You know how Washington weather is. Let's keep going."

Ignoring their instincts, they pressed on, and it got later. The forest seemed to close in around them, the fog thickened, and the whispers of the trees grew louder, more insistent. Shadows danced at the edge of their vision, and the ground seemed to shift beneath their feet.

Suddenly, a high-pitched screeching sound pierced the group, but it affected Jenna the most, like a bolt of lightning with a chorus of a thousand demons screaming in her mind. Jenna cried out, clutching her head. "I can't... I can't take it! They're in my mind!" Her eyes glazed over with terror, she tore off her backpack and she darted off into the thicket of the woods. Chris and Alex scrambled after her, but the forest twisted and turned, leading them astray. Panic set in as they realized they were hopelessly lost.

Jenna stumbled through the underbrush, her mind reeling with whispers of the forest. She fell to her knees, clutching her head, as a sinister voice seethed through her thoughts. It promised release and demanded surrender. But deep within, a flicker of defiance fought to stay alight. Amidst the madness, an apparition appeared, a shadow of a woman draped in sorrow. Her eyes, dark and hollow, met Jenna's with a silent plea of salvation. It whispered "Itami ga kieru," "Tamashī o taberu." Jenna didn't know what she said. But somehow, she understood. Jenna pulled out her pocketknife. Looked down at both her hands, clutching the knife in her right hand, with her left wrist exposed.

Chris and Alex continued their desperate search for Jenna, their fear turning to frustration. The forest seemed to feed on their desperation, whispering twisted thoughts into their minds. Tensions escalated, and as the relentless whispers continued, they turned on each other.

Chris, driven by paranoia, accused Alex of leading them astray. "This is your fault, Alex! You brought us here and now we're gonna die!"

Alex, consumed by his own hallucinations, snapped back. "You're the one who wanted to keep going! We should have turned back!"

The argument quickly escalated into a physical altercation. In a fit of rage, Chris grabbed a rock and struck Alex, the blow sending him sprawling to the ground. Alex's blood oozing from his head seeped into the forest floor, and as the life drained from his body, the ground beneath him began to shift and slither.

The forest, sensing the fresh blood, came alive with a sinister hunger. Roots and tendrils emerged from the ground, wrapping around Alex's body and pulling him into the earth. Chris watched in horror as the forest devoured his friend, the roots burrowing into Alex's flesh, drinking in his remaining life force.

Paralyzed with fear, Chris tried to back away, but the forest wasn't done with him. The whispers screamed louder, more insistent, driving him to the brink of madness. He stumbled, falling to his knees, as the roots turned their attention to him. They snaked around his legs, pulling him towards the ground. He screamed, but his cries were swallowed by the forest.

As the roots tightened their grip, Chris felt his strength fading away. The forest seemed to feed on his terror, growing stronger with each passing moment. The roots pierced his skin, drawing out his life, and as he was pulled into the earth, he realized the terrible truth: the forest consumes the living, using their bodies to sustain its malevolent power. Chris screamed as he was pulled under.

Days later, search parties discovered remnants of a struggle and leftover clothing debris; but the friends were never seen again. Disappearances continue to this day, warning all who dare to enter the Olympic National Forest to stay away. For those who heeded the warning, it was a tale of caution. But for those who ignored it, the forest held an unforgiving truth: the only way to survive was to never venture in.

The Terror of Olympic National Forest

It was a crisp autumn evening when John decided to take his two children, 10-year-old Tommy and 14-year-old Sarah, on a camping trip deep in the Olympic National Forest. They parked their truck and hiked only about 100 yards from it, feeling secure in their proximity to the vehicle.

As they set up camp, the family chatted and joked. John and Tommy pitched the tent while Sarah gathered firewood.

"Dad, do you think we'll see any cool animals?" Tommy asked, his eyes wide with excitement.

"Maybe some deer or raccoons," John replied with a grin. "Just remember to keep our food stored properly so we don't attract any unwanted visitors."

Sarah returned with an armful of wood. "I can't wait to roast marshmallows and tell ghost stories!"

As night fell, they gathered around the crackling campfire. The flames cast dancing shadows on the trees, creating an eerie yet cozy atmosphere. John pulled out a bag of marshmallows, and they all took turns roasting them to golden perfection.

"Okay, who's got a good ghost story?" John asked, his voice taking on a playful, spooky tone.

"I have one!" Sarah exclaimed. "Once upon a time, there was a haunted mining cabin deep in the woods..."

As Sarah spun her tale, Tommy's eyes grew wide, and he clung to his father's arm. "That's so creepy, sis!"

John chuckled. "Great story, Sarah. How about this one?" He leaned in closer to the fire, casting a dramatic shadow on his face. "Long ago, in these very woods, there was a hermit who vanished without a trace. They say his ghost still wanders these parts, searching for something he lost..."

The family laughed and shivered at the spooky stories, feeling a bond of closeness in the shared experience.

As the night wore on, they settled into their tent, unaware of the lurking danger. In the early morning hours, they were abruptly awakened by growls and snarls. A giant, hungry bear had found its way to their campsite.

John sprang into action, trying to protect his children. The bear attacked with ferocity, its massive claws tearing into the tent and smashing down on Sarah's leg, breaking it. She screamed in agony. John confronted the beast, grabbing a nearby branch in a desperate attempt to fend it off. The bear swiped at him with a powerful paw, sending him crashing to the ground.

Tommy screamed in terror as the bear turned its attention to him. It lunged, its jaws closing around the boy's arm. Tommy screamed and passed out from fear and pain. John, bleeding and in agony, managed to pull the bear away from his son, but the beast was relentless. With a savage growl, it knocked John to the ground and bit into his shoulder, John groaned painfully with blood spraying across the campsite.

Sarah, barely able to move with the pain of her injured leg, crawled to her brother. "Tommy, stay with me!" she cried, trying to shake him awake. But Tommy was unconscious, his arm mangled and bleeding profusely.

The bear's attack on John grew more violent, its claws ripping through flesh and muscle. In a desperate bid to save his children, John fought back with all his remaining strength, but the bear was too powerful. With a final, sickening crunch, the bear's jaws clamped down on John's neck, silencing him forever. Just as suddenly as the attack happened, it stopped.

Sarah, her heart pounding, found the cell phone and dialed her mother's number. To her surprise, she managed to get a signal and called Karen.

"Mom! We were attacked by a bear! Dad... Dad is dead, and Tommy is hurt bad. My leg is broken, but the bear left," Sarah cried, her voice trembling with fear.

Karen, helpless and panicking, tried to console her daughter. "Stay strong, Sarah. Help is on the way. Just hold on."

But the relief was short-lived. Sarah's voice suddenly filled with terror. She screamed. "Mom, it's coming back. It has two baby bears with her... Mom, Mom, they're eating me!"

The phone went silent, leaving Karen in a state of unimaginable horror.

Hours later, a rescue party found the campsite and witnessed the tragedy that had occurred. The events that transpired served as a warning to all who ventured into the woods. When you enter the Olympic National Forest, you are stepping into the food chain. It is a cautionary tale for those who heed the warning, and for those who still venture in, always remember to bring your bear spray.

The Forbidden Stairs of a Dark Forest

In the depths of the Olympic National Forest, nestled among the towering trees and thick underbrush, there stood a peculiar set of stairs. No one knows how they got there. They appeared to be from an old, abandoned structure, seemingly leading up to nowhere. The locals knew the legend well: "Don't go near and definitely don't climb on a set of stairs that are randomly in the forest."

On a foggy summer morning, four friends—Ali, Rachel, Mark, and Lisa—decided to go hiking deep into the forest. Mark drove everyone to the end of a long forest service road that led to the trailhead they wanted to explore. They had heard gossip of eerie stairs but dismissed them as mere superstition. Their adventurous spirits and curiosity got the better of them.

"Do you really believe in those old stories?" Ali scoffed as they trudged through the dense foliage.

Rachel shrugged. "I don't know, but it's fun to think about. Maybe we'll find them and see what the fuss is all about."

After hours of hiking, they stumbled upon a clearing where the trees parted, revealing the mysterious stairs. They were made of stone, as if from an ancient castle, covered in moss and vines, leading up a few steps to another world.

"Is this it?" Mark asked, his voice tinged with excitement.

Lisa hesitated. "Maybe we shouldn't... I've heard some really creepy things about these stairs."

But Ali, eager to prove his bravery, ran up the stairs, which were only about 10 steps. When he reached the top, he turned to the others with a blank stare and, in a flat tone, said, "Come on up, guys."

Lisa stepped up a few steps and stopped cold in her tracks, her eyes wide with fear. Just as Mark was about to touch the stairs and join them, Rachel pulled him back. "Don't! Something's wrong," she whispered, her voice trembling.

Suddenly, the ground beneath them began to shake, and the stairs seemed to grow taller, stretching impossibly high. The sky darkened, and an otherworldly mist surrounded them, obscuring their view of the forest.

"What's happening?" Rachel cried, panic rising in her chest.

Before anyone could respond, they heard a haunting whisper, carried on the breeze. It grew louder, filling their minds with dread. The stairs pulsed with an unnatural energy, and the friends felt their bodies being pulled apart, as if they were being torn from reality itself.

Mark clutched his head, his eyes wide with terror. "We need to get out of here!"

But as they tried to take a step, they found themselves unable to move. The whispers grew deafening, and the mist thickened, swallowing them whole. One by one, they vanished into the dense mist, their screams echoing through the forest.

Rachel and Mark awoke from being unconscious for who knows how long. They were sure they were where the stairs had been, but now the stairs, Ali, and Lisa were gone.

Rachel and Mark frantically searched the area, calling out their friends' names, but there was no response. As they searched deeper into the forest, an overwhelming sense of anxiety gripped them, bringing them to the brink of panic.

Hours later, they stumbled upon a clearing where Ali and Lisa stood motionless, their faces blank and expressionless, as if they were in a trance.

"Ali! Lisa!" Rachel cried, but there was no recognition in their eyes.

Mark approached cautiously, his heart pounding. "What's wrong with them?"

As they got closer, they realized Ali and Lisa were mumbling incoherently, their eyes vacant and soulless.

The forest seemed to pulse with a malevolent energy, and the whispers of the trees grew louder, filling their minds with fear.

"We have to get out of here," Rachel urged, pulling Mark away from their entranced friends. "This place is cursed."

But as they tried to leave, the forest twisted and turned, leading them astray. The whispers grew deafening as the supernatural mist thickened, surrounding them, obscuring their view.

Desperate to escape, Rachel and Mark stumbled through the forest, but a malevolent force seemed to follow them, pushing them to the brink of exhaustion. They knew they had to find a way out before the forest claimed them as it had Ali and Lisa.

Miraculously, Rachel and Mark managed to find their way back to the truck and drove to the nearest town, where they alerted the authorities. A rescue party was quickly assembled and sent out to search for the two friends.

Days later, the rescue party found them. Ali was wandering naked and disoriented. Lisa, too, was found naked and was hiding in a burrowed-out tree trunk pulling out her hair. They were forever changed, their eyes empty and soulless, as if the forest had consumed their essence, leaving them vacant and hollow.

The legend of the forbidden stairs grew, warning all that when you looked for the stairs, the forest would stare back and lead you to a place from which there was no return.

Whispers in the Wind

It was Labor Day weekend, and a small group of college friends—Emily, Jake, Laura, and Ben—wanted to have one more adventure before the summer was over. Emily suggested a camping trip near an old mining settlement. They chose a campsite that was rumored to be near a hidden trail that led to the forgotten mining camp, abandoned decades ago under mysterious circumstances. On this moonless night, from their campsite, they embarked on a night hike to explore the heart of the Olympic National Forest.

Armed with flashlights, chem-lights, and a sense of adventure, the small group of college friends ventured deep into the forest. Periodically, they cracked a chem-light and dropped it on the path, hoping to illuminate their way home. The dense canopy above blocked out any remaining light, and the path grew narrower with every step. As they walked, an eerie silence enveloped them, broken only by the rustling of leaves and the occasional distant hoot of an owl. The smell of damp earth and decaying leaves permeated the air, adding to the sense of isolation. Emily had explored this forest during the day on previous trips, so she felt they were safe, but she had never found the mining camp. She wanted to keep her friends in suspense and the anticipation high.

"I can't believe we're doing this," Jake muttered, shaking his head. "My mom would kill me if she knew."

"Relax, Jake," Emily said with a grin. "Where's your sense of adventure?"

"I left it back at camp," Jake replied, glancing nervously around.

"Come on, guys. This is supposed to be fun," Laura chimed in, her excitement evident. "Think of the stories we'll have!"

"Do you think we'll actually find this old settlement?" Ben asked, his voice echoing in the quiet night.

"I hope so," Laura replied. "Imagine the stories we could tell!"

As they continued their journey, the air grew colder, and a thick fog began to roll in, obscuring their path. The forest seemed to close in around them, and an unsettling feeling crept up their spines. The fog was so dense it seemed to have a physical presence, wrapping around them like a ghostly shroud. The chill in the air nipped at their skin, and they could feel the moisture from the fog settling on their faces.

"Guys, do you hear that?" Emily whispered, her ears straining to catch the faintest sound—something she hadn't heard before.

"Hear what?" Laura asked, stopping in her tracks.

"Shh, listen," Emily urged.

The group fell silent, and then they heard it—a soft, haunting whisper carried by the light blowing wind high in the trees. It was incomprehensible, yet it sent shivers down their spines. As they strained to hear more, the whispers grew louder and more persistent, and they could just make out their names being called in the eerie murmur.

"Probably just the wind," Jake said, trying to reassure them, but his own voice trembled with unease.

"Let's keep moving," Ben suggested, though his grip on the flashlight tightened. "We need to find this place before we freak ourselves out."

They pressed on, determined to find the settlement. After what felt like hours, they stumbled upon a clearing. In the center stood the remnants of old wooden structures, barely standing and covered in moss. Next to them was what appeared to be old mining or logging equipment, dilapidated from time. The air was heavy with a sense of foreboding, and the smell of rust and decay hung in the air.

"We found it!" Laura exclaimed, but her excitement was short-lived.

The whispers grew louder, more insistent. The friends looked around, trying to pinpoint the source, but the voices seemed to come from all directions. The fog thickened, and shadows danced in the darkness, creating an eerie illusion of movement.

"Let's take a quick look and get out of here," Ben suggested, his nerves on edge.

"I'm with Ben," Jake said. "This place gives me the creeps."

"Don't be such a scaredy-cat," Laura teased, though she too looked uneasy.

As they explored the decaying buildings, the whispers grew deafening. Emily stumbled upon an old journal, its pages yellowed with age. Curious, she opened it and began to read aloud:

"They came in the night, their whispers driving us to madness. We tried to flee, but the forest would not let us go. We are trapped, forever lost among the whispers of the wind."

Suddenly, the ground beneath them began to tremble, and the shadows seemed to come alive. The friends' flashlights flickered and died, plunging them into darkness. Panic set in as the whispers grew unbearably loud, echoing in their minds.

Laura screamed, "I can't take it anymore!" Everyone was clasping their heads, screaming in pain. The trembling ground grew stronger and roared.

Just then, they saw what looked like an older woman dressed in a gown, holding a lantern, directing them to come her way.

"That way, run!" Jake shouted. He ran first, and the others followed, running as fast as they could toward where the woman was directing them. One by one, they vanished into the mist, their screams echoing through the forest.

Days later, a search party found their lifeless bodies at the bottom of an abandoned mine shaft, never knowing what truly happened. The discovery of their bodies only fueled the rumors and mystery surrounding the forgotten settlement. Despite the numerous search efforts and investigations, the events that led up to their deaths remained unexplained. The local community was left in shock and fear, and many residents became wary of venturing too deep into the forest.

The legend of the hidden trail and the abandoned mining camp became a cautionary tale, passed down through generations. Visitors to the Olympic National Forest would hear the story, around campfires and shared with trepidation. It served as a chilling reminder of the forest's dark history, a mystery that many dared not explore.

Some say that on moonless nights, the whispers still echo through the trees, a ghostly warning to those who dare to wander off the beaten path. For those who have heard the tale and respect its warning, the forest remains a place of natural beauty. But for the curious and the brave, the forest holds a sinister secret—a reminder that some trails are best left forgotten.

Lake Crescent Monster

On a misty overcast autumn morning, under the canopy of towering evergreens, three seasoned fishermen—Joe, Tom, and Rick—set out on Lake Crescent in search of the largest trout they had ever seen. They are called Beardslee Lunkers, an almost mythical fish that can grow to the size of half the length of a man. Lake Crescent is an ancient lake; its creation story is full of folklore and legend. With one look at this lake, you would think that all of the stories are true. The lake was serene, its surface like a mirror reflecting the towering trees and the overcast sky above.

The barometer was dropping, indicating inclement weather. Despite this, Joe knew these were the best conditions for fishing. He wanted to try out his brand-new 19-foot fiberglass outboard, and what better way to have a maiden voyage than to share it with friends?"

The fishing was great that day, with almost every cast resulting in a catch. They kept only the biggest ones and let the smaller ones, which were at least 15 inches long, go. By no means were these small fish.

"It's like the fish want to jump in our boat!" Tom exclaimed, searching for another lure.

"Can't keep'em all, I'm here for the Lunkers," Rick replied, holding his fishing pole at the ready.

"Must be a monster scaring them out of the lake," Tom joked, and everyone laughed.

"Has anyone ever heard of the Crescent Lake legend?" Joe asked, gazing out over the water. Tom and Rick replied, "No."

"Well, legend has it that there are deep caverns that go through the lakebed into the Strait of Juan de Fuca. Prehistoric sea monsters that can breathe both fresh and sea water, like salmon, swim through these caves back to Lake Crescent to lay their eggs. They say this lake is an ancient prehistoric breeding ground," Joe explained.

Tom and Rick laughed, "That's ridiculous! Where did you hear that?" Rick blurted out.

"That salty old man at the gas station. He told it to me when I was getting gas for the boat while you guys were inside getting snacks." Joe replied.

"Well, as long as he's been around, it's probably true," Tom chuckled. Everyone laughed.

The day carried on and everyone almost caught their limit. There was nothing under 30 inches in the hold. The weather seemed to be getting worse. The sky was darkening. The air was getting colder. A fog was rolling in, dancing on the surface of the lake like an elegant ice skater.

As they drifted further into the lake, an eerie silence fell. The usual chorus of frogs and crickets had gone mysteriously quiet. Tom, sensing something was off, cast a worried glance toward his friends, who were engrossed in their fishing gear.

"Hey, do you guys hear that?" Tom whispered, his voice trembling slightly.

"Hear what?" Joe replied, not looking up from his line.

"Exactly. It's too quiet," Tom muttered, scanning the dark waters around them.

The boat rocked gently, a small wave lapping against the side. Rick, the joker of the group, grinned. "Relax, Tom. Maybe the fish just know we're coming for 'em."

But Tom couldn't shake his unease. He reached for his flashlight, aiming its beam into the depths of the lake. Just then, an unusually large shadow passed underneath them.

"Did you see that?" Tom gasped, gripping the flashlight tightly.

Joe and Rick peered over the edge with Tom, their faces pale in the dim light. "What the hell was that?" Joe whispered, his voice barely audible.

Before they could react, the boat lurched violently, rocking side to side, nearly tossing them overboard. A chilling growl resonated from the depths, sending a shiver down their spines.

"We need to get out of here!" Joe shouted, fumbling with the boat's engine. But the motor sputtered and died, leaving them stranded in the middle of the lake.

"It must have hit the prop shaft," Joe barked. "What the hell is that?" Tom screamed and pointed.

The creature circled them, its eyes glowing like fiery embers in the water. Each pass it made brought it closer, its monstrous form breaking the surface with a sickening gurgle.

"Row! We have to row!" Rick yelled, grabbing an oar.

They paddled furiously, but the creature was faster, more determined. It lunged again, its teeth tearing into the boat, taking a massive bite out of the stern. The fishermen scrambled to the front, their hearts pounding. It came back around and smashed into the starboard side.

"This can't be happening," Joe muttered, his voice a mixture of fear and disbelief. They were huddled in the front of the boat, Rick closest to the edge.

Just then, a creature leaped out of the water over the boat. It was a monstrous, nightmarish beast, with scales that glistened like wet obsidian in what little light they had. The creature's eyes blazed with fury, and its body was a grotesque fusion of crocodile and shark with a long, sinuous tail that thrashed the water into a frenzy. Its massive jaws, lined with rows of razor-sharp teeth, snapped Rick in half with a sickening crunch, spewing blood everywhere before splashing back into the water on the other side.

Joe and Tom screamed at each other, "Rick! Oh my God, Oh my God! What was that? I don't know. It was hideous!"

The boat was taking on water. The sky turned pitch black, and the fog wasn't so pretty to them now.

They heard the surface of the water break. It was coming back for more.

The next morning, local authorities found their boat, floating aimlessly near the shore. The once-sturdy vessel now bore the scars of a brutal encounter—deep, jagged teeth marks that told a tale of terror. Tom, Joe, and Rick were never found or heard from again, their disappearance shrouded in mystery.

To this day, locals speak in hushed tones about the legend of Lake Crescent, warning those who dare venture out. They say a monster still lurks beneath the surface, waiting for its next victims.

So, the next time you're near Lake Crescent, remember the tale of the three fishermen and the creature that claimed their lives. And if you ever hear the water surface break on an otherwise calm day, it might be best to back away and stay ashore.

The Hot Springs of Doom

It was a crisp early autumn morning, the kind that promised adventure with its cool air and clear skies. A group of friends—Jamal, Emma, Colton, and Leah—had heard rumors about a hidden gem in the Olympic National Forest: a secluded natural hot spring that was said to be like a magical jacuzzi.

Determined to experience this wonder, they found the location, mapped out their route and set off. They drove to the trailhead, which was at the end of a long logging road. The scenery on the hike was perfect—sunshine filtering through the canopy of old-growth trees, some leaves crunching underfoot, and the scent of pine filling the air. Laughter and chatter echoed through the woods as they made their way through the forest.

Two hours into the hike, they arrived. The sight was breathtaking—a serene pool of steaming water nestled among moss-covered rocks, with a light chorus of bubbles breaking the surface, merging harmoniously with the rustling leaves and distant birdsongs. The air was alive with a soothing hint of nourishing minerals and sulfur. The hot spring was everything they had hoped for.

"Can you believe we finally made it?" Emma said, her eyes sparkling with excitement.

"This place is amazing; I can't wait to get in." Jamal replied, grinning.

"I'm going to change; no peaking boys." Leah said with a smile.

They all quickly changed into their bathing suits, shivering in the cool air, but the promise of warm water was too inviting to resist.

The rocks were slippery, but one by one, they managed to ease themselves into the hot spring, the heat enveloping them like a warm embrace.

"Ah, this is the life," Colton sighed, leaning back with a contented smile.

"Totally worth the hike," Leah added, her eyes closed as she soaked in the warmth.

They leaned back, neck-deep in the soothing water, sharing jokes and stories, their voices mingling with the gentle bubbling of the spring. As they laughed, the bubbling became more pronounced. The temperature rose slightly, but they dismissed it as a natural occurrence, joking about the "self-heating jacuzzi."

"The spring knows we're here," Jamal said with a chuckle. "It's giving us the VIP treatment."

The tranquility of the moment was short-lived. Without warning, the ground beneath them began to tremble and shake violently.

The towering trees swayed dangerously, while the once-peaceful hot spring roared fiercely, as if stirred by a growl from the depths below.

"Earthquake!" Colton yelled, panic flashing in his eyes. They scrambled to escape, but the slippery rocks betrayed them. The quaking ground and the unstable footing sent them back into the scalding water. The temperature soared, turning the once-inviting pool into a boiling cauldron.

"Help! I can't get out!" Emma screamed, her voice filled with terror.

"Jamal! Colton!" Leah cried, her voice choked with pain as the boiling water consumed her.

The water seared, causing blisters and burns. The intense heat melted their skin. Their screams echoed through the forest, an excruciating symphony of agony and despair.

Their bodies thrashing one last time before going still. Within moments, they were tragically silenced.

The next day, a park ranger on routine patrol found their abandoned car at the trailhead. Concerned, he hiked up to the hot springs to investigate. As he approached, a strange, unsettling smell filled the air, like cooking stew but with an odd, unsettling undertone.

When he reached the hot spring, the sight that greeted him was horrifying. The once-pristine waters were now a gruesome broth, and the bodies of the friends lay still in the superheated pool. The ranger's heart sank, a chill running down his spine despite the heat. The hot springs had turned from a natural wonder to a human stew. They were boiled alive.

The Lost Treasure of Captain Kendrick

In 1791, Captain John Kendrick embarked on an ambitious voyage from Hawaii to China, seeking to trade furs. His journey led him to a notorious smugglers' cove known as Dirty Butter Bay, the only place in China suitable for his trade. After completing his business there, Kendrick set his sights on Japan, hoping to establish trade relations. However, the Japanese were not keen on foreign traders and drove him away with a show of armed samurai.

Unbeknownst to Captain Kendrick, a band of Chinese pirates had been trailing him. As he sailed to the south side of Hokkaido, the pirates launched a surprise attack on his ship, the Lady Washington, aiming to seize its riches and make a quick escape through the Sea of Japan. However, the pirates underestimated Kendrick's strategic prowess and the longer range of the Lady Washington's cannons. The pirates were swiftly defeated, and their vessel was stripped of all provisions. Amidst the chaos, Kendrick discovered a bounty of Chinese imperial gold and treasures, which he concealed among his cargo before sending the surviving pirates adrift and scuttling their ship.

Upon reaching the Canadian coastal island of Haida Gwaii to replenish fresh water and supplies, Kendrick encountered an embittered ex-chief named Koyah. A fierce battle ensued, and Koyah was ultimately defeated. With his treasure intact, Kendrick sailed for Nootka Bay, a previously neutral territory. However, wary of the shifting political landscape and his recent ordeal, Kendrick decided to make a stop at Shi-Shi Beach to hide the imperial treasure. On a foggy morning, with only two crewmen by his side, Kendrick unloaded the treasure and hid it beyond the sea stacks in the harsh foothills surrounding the beach.

Kendrick then continued to the Nootka Trading Camp, which had been commandeered by the Spanish. Despite the change in control, he was welcomed and able to rest, replenish his supplies, and make necessary repairs. A month later, as he sailed past Neah Bay, just north of Shi-Shi Beach, he noticed a Spanish ship preparing surveys of the area. He had learned at Nootka Trading Camp that the Spanish intended to establish a trading post at Neah Bay. Deciding it was best not to draw attention, Kendrick sailed on to Hawaii, confident that the treasure was well hidden.

Over the years, Captain Kendrick continued his trade, navigating the Pacific Trade Triangle between Hawaii, China, and the Pacific Northwest. He became a successful and legendary figure in the trading world. However, the imperial Chinese treasure he buried among the rugged terrain of Shi-Shi Beach remains untouched. The beach's name, Shi-Shi, meaning 'Surf Beach' in the Native

American language and 'Imperial Guardian Lion' in Chinese, seem fitting guardians, as the waves crash upon the shore, forever watching over the lost treasure of Captain Kendrick.

The Lost Englishman's Gold Mine

In the late 1800s, Silas Marple, an explorer and adventurer from Brennan, Washington, ventured into the dense, mist-shrouded expanse of the Olympic National Forest. The forest, with its towering evergreens and lush undergrowth, was a place of both beauty and danger. During his exploration, Silas discovered an area rich in copper and manganese. Enthusiastic about his find, he filed a mining claim and rallied investors to fund the mining operation, forming the Tubal Cain Copper and Manganese Mining Company. News of the discovery spread like wildfire, and within a year, the once-quiet forest was teeming with explorers and prospectors eager to strike it rich.

However, the mining venture proved to be a rigorous and unforgiving endeavor. The deposits were not as abundant as initially thought, and the harsh conditions of the forest took their toll on the workers. Disheartened and penniless, the miners abandoned the site, and the camp fell into disrepair. Silas, undeterred by this setback, continued his explorations deeper into the heart of the forest, driven by a hunch of untold riches hidden within.

Legend has it that during one of his solitary expeditions, Silas stumbled upon a hidden gold vein, glittering beneath the canopy of ancient trees along the rugged outcrop of a mountain wall, concealed behind two imposing boulders.

Realizing the immense value of his find, he chose to keep it a closely guarded secret. He remembered the chaos and competition that followed his previous discovery and knew that filing a mining claim would attract unwanted attention. To protect his secret, Silas devised a plan to mine the gold discreetly.

He began taking different routes into the forest, carefully covering his tracks and ensuring no one followed him. Disguising himself as a humble woodsman, he would venture into the deep woods, often vanishing for weeks at a time. Silas returned with satchels full of gold ore, which he sold quietly in small quantities, never at the same establishment, and just enough to sustain himself. He lived a modest and frugal life, never revealing the true extent of his wealth or the location of his secret mine.

As the years passed, Silas grew older, his once-vigorous body worn down by the harsh wilderness. On his deathbed, he confided in his cousin, who had been taking care of him in his final days. With a frail hand, Silas handed over a tattered map and whispered the mine's location, claiming it could make 100 men millionaires. His final words hinted at the immense wealth hidden within the west side of the Olympic mountain range.

Shortly after Silas's passing, rumors of the Lost Englishman's Gold Mine spread throughout the region, fueled by tales of dark black sand on the beaches of the northwest coast, containing gold dust from mountain erosion and runoff. Treasure hunters and adventurers flocked to the area, each hoping to uncover the legendary mine. However, the forest, with its dense undergrowth and treacherous terrain, guarded its secrets well.

A few years after Silas' death, hikers and campers began reporting sightings of a mysterious hermit on the west side of the Olympic Mountain Forest, near the town of Forks. The figure was often seen wandering deep within the woods, near the headwaters of the Sol Duc, Bogachiel and the Hoh Rivers. Some believed it was the ghost of Silas Marple, forever tending to his mine. Others speculated that it was his cousin, tirelessly searching for the treasure that had eluded him.

To this day, one thing remains certain: the legend of the Lost Englishman's Gold Mine endures. The ghostly figure continues to be seen, a phantom presence in the forest's shadowy depths. Locals keep the story alive with campfire tales and eerie anecdotes, drawing curious adventurers to the area. The legend is further fueled by an ancient curse said to protect the treasure, with ghostly apparitions, eerie sounds, and cryptic clues hidden in a tattered old map, adding to the mystery.

Every year, the legend grows, inspiring new generations of treasure hunters to venture into the Olympic National Forest in search of the elusive gold. The forest, with its timeless beauty and haunting atmosphere, remains a place of wonder and intrigue, where the past and present intertwine in the quest for the Lost Englishman's Gold Mine.

Goblins Gate: The Tale of the Mountain King

When the earth was young, billions of years ago, just after the planet had formed and long before humans were even a teardrop in the eye of the Divine, there existed a land of unparalleled beauty and majesty. This land was ruled by the Mountain King, a benevolent and wise ruler whose kingdom was as mystical and mythical as the imagination could hold. The name of these lands was incomprehensible to the human tongue, but its beauty was undeniable.

The Mountain King's kingdom was a realm of peace and righteousness, where lush forests, crystal-clear rivers, and towering mountains reigned supreme. The Mountain King ensured that his lands remained pristine, and all creatures lived in harmony. It was a place where the air was pure, the waters sparkling, and the scenery breathtaking.

But one fateful day, from the depths of the sea, there arose a band of giant goblins. These goblins were ten stories tall and believed themselves to be the mightiest creatures in the land. They decided to claim the Mountain King's kingdom for themselves, convinced that their sheer size granted them the right to rule.

The Mountain King, ever hopeful, watched these creatures from his lofty throne. He hoped that the goblins could become the new stewards of his lands, caring for them with the same love and respect he had always shown. However, as time went on, the Mountain King witnessed the atrocities committed by the goblins. They tore up the land, destroyed the beautiful trees, and burrowed deep into the mountain, disrupting its delicate balance.

Angered and desperate to protect his beloved lands, the Mountain King reached up to the heavens. A fierce storm ensued, and the sky darkened with swirling clouds. With a mighty roar, he summoned a bolt of lightning, a weapon forged from the very essence of his furious anger. The Mountain King cast the lightning bolt at the goblins, piercing each one with its searing energy.

In an instant, the goblins were turned to stone, their massive forms frozen in eternal vigilance. Encased in stone, the goblins now stood as sentinels, guarding the Mountain King's majestic lands for all eternity. The place where this dramatic transformation occurred became known as Goblins Gate, a narrow gorge on the Elwha River within what is now Olympic National Park.

The goblins, once destructive forces, were now immovable protectors of the land.

In the time of humans, Goblins Gate became a place of legend and folklore.

The faces of the goblins, with their anguished features, seemed to silently warn all who passed by of the importance of being good stewards of the land.

Today, Goblins Gate remains a testament to the Mountain King's resolve to protect his kingdom. It serves as a reminder to all who visit to cherish and respect the land. When you pass through Goblins Gate, remember the tale of the Mountain King and the stone goblins. Pick up any trash you may see, leave nothing behind, and do your part to maintain the beauty and harmony of this enchanting place. For if you don't, the goblins may come back to life and take you at night, encasing you in stone to forever watch over this land.

The goblins, though frozen in stone, still guard over this domain with unwavering vigilance, ensuring that the Mountain King's kingdom remains as majestic as it was in the days of old.

The Legend of Mount Storm King

Long ago, in a time before humans recorded history, there lived a gentle king, a loving king, a peaceful king who resided within a majestic mountain. This king, known to his realm as the Mountain King, watched over the land with benevolence and wisdom. As the years passed, humans began to migrate to the area along the shores of the Strait of Juan de Fuca, between what is currently known as Neah Bay and Port Townsend.

These early settlers eventually divided into two tribes—the Tribe of the East and the Tribe of the West. For many centuries, peace reigned over the land. The tribes coexisted harmoniously, and the Mountain King was delighted to see such kindness and cooperation among the people. However, as populations grew, the two tribes began quarreling over hunting territory and exclusive rights to resources, leading to tension between the tribes.

The Mountain King watched cautiously as the tribes began to take a different path. Despite still having abundant resources available to both tribes, the people started to argue over hunting grounds and fishing waters. Skirmishes escalated into small raiding campaigns, with each tribe striving to claim all the resources for themselves.

Eventually, the two tribes gathered their forces in the shadow of the Mountain King. They attacked one another, creating a horrific scene of war, battle, and gore. The Mountain King, enraged by the jealousy, greed, and lack of diplomacy displayed by the tribes, decided to put an end to the violence.

With a mighty roar, the Mountain King sheared off a portion of his mountain and cast it down upon the warring armies. The immense piece of rock crushed the combatants and blocked the flow of the rivers, creating two new lakes—Lake Crescent and the smaller Lake Sutherland.

In the aftermath of this catastrophic event, the Mountain King was forever known as Mount Storm King, a name that carried the weight of his fury and his resolve to protect the land. The bodies of the fallen warriors were never recovered and are said to remain at the bottom of the lakes to this very day. On foggy, moonlit nights, some say that they can see the ghostly apparitions of the two tribal armies engaged in a warlike dance on the surface of the lake.

To this day, the descendants of the tribes view Lake Crescent as a sacred place, one deserving of respect and reverence. They tell the tale of Mount Storm King to remind others of the importance of harmony and the consequences of greed and conflict.

Modern Native Americans honor the legend by treating the area around Mount Storm King and Lake Crescent with the utmost respect. They believe that the spirits of the fallen warriors linger in the waters and that the Mountain King's presence still looms over the land, ensuring that peace is maintained.

When you visit Lake Crescent, remember the tale of Mount Storm King and the creation of the lakes. Cherish the beauty of the land, pick up any trash you may see, and leave nothing behind. Most importantly, be kind to one another. For if you do not, the spirits of the fallen may rise from the depths, and Mount Storm King may once again unleash his wrath upon those who dare to disrupt the harmony of his kingdom.

The Curse of Humes Cabin

The hike to the lookout in Olympic National Forest was supposed to be a long, yet rewarding journey. Midway, the group of hikers stumbled upon Humes Cabin, a quaint dwelling nestled deep in the woods with a 100-year-old apple tree standing proudly in front. The cabin, seemingly untouched by time, piqued their curiosity.

Inside, the air was thick with the scent of history. The hikers laughed and joked as they explored the cabin's rustic interior. James, one of the hikers, stepped on a loose floorboard and instinctively lifted it. Beneath, he found an old, dusty journal.

"Guys, check this out," James called, waving the journal. They gathered around, intrigued.

The journal recounted the lives of the cabin's former inhabitants: a husband named Dave, his wife Elizabeth, and her brother Mike. The entries started with mundane details, but then one day, an enigmatic traveler named Lucas Nox, affectionately known as Nox, visited the cabin. A jovial character, Nox, said he was on a two-week hike exploring the area and spoke of a beautiful lookout at the end of the trail. Before he left, he entrusted them with a small scroll, asking them to keep it safe until his return in four days. He didn't want the scroll damaged on his trip.

They agreed, and as he left, he plucked an apple from the tree. The hikers read the account from the journal.

"We've never had a visitor like Nox before. He seems genuinely kind," Dave remarked, setting the scroll on the table.

"I agree. And that scroll, it must be important if he trusted us with it," Elizabeth responded, her curiosity evident.

"Yeah, but I'm curious what's inside. Should we open it?" Mike suggested, a mischievous glint in his eye.

The journal entries took a dark turn when curiosity overcame the cabin's occupants the next day.

"Maybe it's a treasure map," speculated Mike.

They decided to open the scroll. Inside, they found a single verse in a foreign language.

"Let's see," Dave said, reading aloud, "Expergiscere, kakó katoikídio meum, veni cruciare, consume tuam praemium."

As the words echoed through the cabin, the ground trembled, and a high-pitched noise pierced their ears. A distant growl, carried by the wind, followed.

"What was that? Maybe just an earthquake," Dave suggested nervously.

Over the next three days, the journal detailed their torment by a mysterious creature. It began with taps on the outside of cabin walls and rocks being hurled from the woods. Desperate, the group yelled and threw the rocks back into the darkness. Dave even chased the creature, only to return uneasy and visibly shaken, but he never spoke about what happened. They huddled together in the cabin, discussing what to do. Mike recounted a tale of a mischievous forest monster, the Wendigo, and thought he knew how to kill it with steel and iron, realizing that their lead bullets would be useless against this type of creature. They armed themselves with steel knives, determined to defend themselves.

Suddenly, a deafening roar echoed through the cabin, shaking the very foundations. The creature emerged from the shadows of the woods and began advancing, a grotesque amalgamation of flesh and bone, its eyes glowing with violent intent. Their breaths caught in their throats as they saw the monstrous being through the cabin windows. They began to quickly bar the door, but it was no use—it burst through the cabin door, almost knocking the door completely off its hinges.

Dave lunged first, his steel knife gleaming in the dim light. He slashed at the creature, but it moved with unnatural speed, dodging his attack and retaliating with a swipe of its clawed hand. Dave was thrown against the wall, blood oozing from a gash on his arm, groaning in pain.

"Ahhhhh!" Elizabeth screamed, brandishing her knife. She thrust it into the creature's side, eliciting a guttural snarl. The creature's wound began to heal almost instantly, its flesh knitting together before their eyes.

"It's regenerating!" Mike shouted. "We need to aim for its head!"

The creature lunged at Elizabeth, but Mike tackled it from the side, driving his knife into its neck. The creature howled in pain, thrashing wildly as it tried to shake him off.

The creature's movements became more erratic, its growls turning into pained murmurs.

With a surge of adrenaline, Dave picked himself up and grabbed a nearby iron fire poker. He swung it with all his might, aiming for the creature's head. The impact sent a deafening thwack through the air, and the creature staggered, dazed.

"Now! Finish it!" Dave yelled.

Elizabeth and Mike lunged simultaneously, their knives plunging into the creature's skull. The creature let out a final, anguished roar before collapsing to the ground, its body convulsing before finally lying still.

Breathing heavily, they stood over the fallen creature, their hands and clothes stained with its dark, viscous blood. They exchanged glances, the gravity of their situation settling in.

"We did it," Elizabeth whispered, her voice trembling. "We actually killed it."

"Let's hope it stays dead," Dave replied grimly.

Just as they began to catch their breath, the creature's body twitched. Its eyes snapped open, now glowing with an even fiercer intensity. With a guttural roar, it sprang to its feet, its wounds sealing themselves with terrifying speed.

"It's not dead!" Mike shouted, his voice tinged with panic.

The creature, now more furious than ever, let out a bone-chilling screech and charged at the trio. They hardly had time to react before it barreled past them, smashing through the barely hanging cabin door and disappearing into the woods.

Breathing heavily and clutching their weapons, the group stared at the shattered door, the sounds of the creature's retreat fading into the distance.

"It's supposed to be dead. Wendigos die from steel. I don't know what that is!" Mike exclaimed, stunned.

"We can't go on like this. We need to find a way to stop this creature," Elizabeth said, her voice quivering with fear.

"I'm not sure what else we can do. We've tried everything," Dave replied, frustration lining his face.

"There has to be something. Maybe we can trap it," Mike suggested, his tone determined.

The final entry, written by Elizabeth, described their plan for a last stand. She also wrote that if anyone found this journal, then they didn't make it. She hid the journal under the floorboards, warning future readers never to recite the cryptic words aloud: "Expergiscere, kakó katoikídio meum, veni cruciare, consume tuam praemium," lest they suffer the same fate.

As the hikers finished reading the diary, a chill ran down their spines.

"Oh, my goodness, everyone who lived here died or was eaten by a monster! There isn't another entry," Anne whispered, her voice trembling.

James scoffed, "This isn't true! It's just a story to scare children."

"What was in that scroll?" asked Marlee.

"I don't know, some phrase," Scott began, unwittingly reciting aloud, "Expergiscere, kakó katoikídio meum, veni cruciare, consume tuam praemium."

In that moment, the ground began to tremble, a high-pitched noise pierced their ears, and a distant roar echoed through the forest. The hikers stared at each other in shock and terror, realizing they had just unleashed the creature upon themselves.

Batsquatch: The Midnight Hunt

It was in the afternoon, and spring was giving way to summer. My dad, always eager to hunt, insisted on going out. This wasn't a father-son bonding trip; he was out there poaching, indifferent to what he shot. The deer were either still pregnant or rearing their young, but he didn't care.

I was 10 years old, and my dad was an abusive man, especially when drunk. My mom worked as a waitress at the local diner in the small town of Forks. We lived outside of town, with no neighbors, so no one noticed the beatings he gave us. My mom, my little brother, and I endured it all. She probably stayed because she had no other options. Anyway, he said we needed to put food on the table, so we went poaching.

He always made me carry all the gear: his beer, whiskey flask, and rifle. We loaded up in his old blue Dodge pickup—rifle, beer, booze, and smokes—and headed down Forest Road 29. You could get lost back there, with roads veering off in different directions. We drove deep into the woods, and I was terrified, not of the woods, but sitting next to the scariest thing I knew: my dad.

It was still early, with some daylight left, but it was late afternoon when we parked off the side of the road. We were so deep in the woods, and there was no one around. We climbed up a small hill and looked down into a little valley. It wasn't a big clearing, but enough to see if anything came through. We sat there in silence, except for his smoking and drinking. His heavy breathing and the clinking of beer bottles were the only constant sounds.

"Keep quiet, boy," he growled, taking a swig of whiskey from his flask. "You'll scare off all the game." I kept my mouth shut and tried to stay warm.

As time passed, we didn't see much. He coughed and scolded me, blaming me for being too loud. I was used to it and just stayed quiet, trying not to get beaten again. As we were losing light, we needed to head back to the truck before it got completely dark. I gathered our belongings, picking up after him as he left his beer bottles everywhere.

It was almost pitch black when we got back to the truck, but the moon was rising, giving us some light. We started up the truck and headed back down the old dirt road.

The forest was a labyrinth of shadows, with the flickering moonlight barely piercing through the dense canopy. The headlights of the truck cast eerie shapes on the trees, and as we made our way back, the darkness seemed to close in around us as we navigated the dirt road.

After a couple of miles, the engine sputtered and stalled. He tried to start it again, but it wouldn't turn back on. He got out, cursing, and blamed me for everything. "What did you do, you little idiot?" he shouted. "Did you forget to put gas in the tank?"

"The gas tank is half full," I said quietly.

"I should have never had kids," he muttered under his breath. He popped the hood and wiggled a few wires, but it didn't help. He grabbed the rifle and told me to hand him a beer. "Don't talk back to me, boy." He gave me a good smack after I handed him the beer. Then he said we had to walk.

The scent of pine and damp earth filled the air. I could smell the alcohol on his breath, a pungent reminder of his unpredictable temper. The night air was bitter cold, seeping through my jacket. The metallic taste of fear lingered in my mouth, a constant companion on nights he heavily drank. The occasional rustle of leaves and distant calls of nocturnal animals added to the unnerving silence of the night.

We got about 100 yards from the truck when he realized he'd forgotten his smokes. He patted his pockets, but they weren't there. He turned me around and started digging through the backpack I was wearing, but they weren't in there either. "You idiot! You left my smokes." Furious, he blamed me for forgetting his cigarettes, smacking and kicking me to the ground.

 "Stop!" I groaned, curled up in a ball as he attacked me. We suddenly heard a screech so loud it echoed through the entire forest. It sounded like a giant eagle. He stopped kicking me, and we both looked around. Then, a huge creature landed next to us. It was 10 feet tall with enormous, bat-like wings. Its body was covered in coarse, matted fur. Its hands were gigantic and sharp, resembling those of a gorilla, with claws. Its legs were powerful, with muscles rippling beneath its fur, ending in talons that dug into the earth. Its head was like that of a wolf, with eyes that glowed a haunting yellow. Its gaze was both captivating and terrifying, filled with a primal intelligence.

The creature let out a guttural growl that sent shivers down my spine. The sound was a mixture of a wolf's snarl and a predatory bird's screech. It looked at me, then at my dad. We were frozen, unable to move.

"What the hell is that?" my dad whispered, his voice trembling.

The creature swiped at him with lightning speed, its claws tearing through his jacket and sending him flying to the ground. His rifle flew into the bushes, lost in the darkness.

The creature looked back at me, its yellow eyes glowing with an eerie intensity. Then, it turned towards my dad, who was on his back, trying to scoot away in fear. With two powerful steps, the creature reached him. It grabbed him by the neck and chest, lifting him effortlessly off the ground. My dad's eyes were wide with terror, and he struggled helplessly in the creature's grip.

"No, please!" he begged, his voice breaking. "Don't kill me!"

Before I could even scream, the creature spread its massive wings and took off into the air with my dad still in its grasp. The sound of the wings flapping was like thunder, echoing through the forest. Under the moonlight, I saw the creature rise higher and higher, until it was a silhouette against the moon.

Then, with a brutal motion, the creature tore him in two, like snapping a twig. Blood and gore rained down, and the creature carried the two halves of him in each hand, flying away into the darkness. I never saw it again or heard anything else.

Terrified and in shock, I got up from the ground and ran back to the truck and locked myself inside. My dad had the keys in his pocket, so I couldn't start the truck. I stayed there until the sun came up, too scared to move. Eventually, I gathered my courage and walked back to town, reaching it by nighttime. I got help, and my mom was a nervous wreck, worried about us.

I didn't tell anyone about the creature. I said that we were out poaching, the truck stopped working, and my dad went to get help while I stayed in the truck. When he didn't return by morning, I decided to walk back to town.

The sheriff found signs of a struggle near the truck but no sign of my dad. He concluded it was a bear attack and filed his report.

Before leaving, the sheriff whispered to me, "Your mom's a nice woman. Maybe this is for the best. He never gave you a chance." I didn't understand then, but now I have a family of my own, and I treat my kids with love and respect. Sometimes, I wonder if I really saw what I saw. Some people talk about a creature called Batsquatch, a terrifying beast with bat-like wings and the body of a sasquatch. Was Batsquatch there protecting me, or was I just on the ground and didn't seem like a threat in that moment? I like to think he was protecting me. They say your mind can play tricks on you, but every so often, I think about that night in the woods and wonder if Batsquatch is real.

The Phantom Camper

My friends and I decided to go camping. Winter was breaking and spring was giving way. The crisp air carried a hint of damp earth and the scent of pine needles. It was still chilly out, especially at night. We planned to do a bit of car camping and some recreational hiking during the day, so we camped at a trailhead. We set up our tents, gathered firewood and got the camp all set up.

That evening, we laughed, joked, and told stories over dinner. The warm glow of the fire danced on our faces as we huddled close to fend off the night's chill. We had a delicious pot of campfire stew in the Dutch oven hanging above the fire on a tripod. The savory aroma of simmering meat and vegetables filled the air, making our mouths water. The wind occasionally blew smoke in our faces. It was good to be out of the city. Everything was perfect.

"Man, this stew is amazing! Your secret recipe, Max?" Matt asked, savoring another spoonful.

Max grinned. "You know it! Just a little bit of this and that. Glad you like it."

Then, we heard someone approaching. We were quite far from civilization, but we heard a voice say, "Hello?" from just outside the firelight. It was dark, and there wasn't much moonlight, making it hard to see who it was. A figure of a young man stepped into the firelight, revealing a college-aged person who was nice in appearance.

"I've been out hiking all day and saw your fire. I was wondering if I could sit by and get warm," he said, his voice was soft, almost pleading.

"Of course! Here, have some stew. It's fresh and hot," Jay offered, extending a bowl.

"Thank you so much. It smells good and will really hit the spot," the stranger said, taking a seat and eagerly accepting the bowl.

As he ate, we noticed he didn't have much gear with him—no sleeping bag, no backpack, just a nice outdoor coat, boots, and pants. His attire seemed a bit dated, but well-kept, so we figured it was just his style. We all sat around the fire, the crackling flames casting long shadows. We shared stories of our adventures, the sound of our laughter mingling with the evening sounds of the forest. We steered clear of politics and focused on more enjoyable topics. Our new friend began telling us tales of the area, his voice a low, mesmerizing cadence. He spoke of logging and hunting adventures, ghost stories, folklore, and tall tales that sent shivers down our spines. The hours passed and it was getting late. Just as he had our complete, undivided attention he leaned in and said;

"There's a legend about a logger who went missing in these woods. Some say his spirit still roams here, looking for his lost axe," his eyes glinting in the firelight.

Just then, we heard a loud snap behind us, like a large twig or branch breaking. The sudden noise shattered our trance-like state. Startled, we grabbed and shined our flashlights in that direction but saw nothing. The beam of light cut through the darkness, revealing only the swaying branches. When we turned back to the fire, our friend was gone. We shined our flashlights all around, the beams darting frantically through the trees, but there was no sign of him. It was impossible for him to have left so quickly and silently. We called out to him, but there was no response. Interestingly, none of us had gotten his name. The bowl of stew he had been eating from was empty and sitting next to where he had been.

"What the heck? Where did he go?" Matt asked, looking around in bewilderment.

"He couldn't have just vanished... could he?" Jay added, his voice tinged with unease.

Perplexed and more than a little startled, we tried to shrug off the incident and turned in for the night. The next morning, everything seemed normal, except for one thing. Where our visitor had been sitting, there was what appeared to be a small index card. I picked it up and realized it was an old black-and-white photo of a group of men in a shack, their faces stern and worn. They looked like loggers from the turn of the century. To the far right of the picture, there was a young man—handsome, with no beard or mustache. It was our visitor from the night before.

Campsite Ghost

It was late summer, early autumn when a young couple, Kevin and Emma, decided to go camping. Kevin knew of a secluded place where they could drive and camp right from the car. The views were beautiful, with magnificent sunrises and sunsets. They gathered up all their gear and drove out there. It was early afternoon when they arrived.

They set up camp, pitched their tent, and got hungry, so they made sandwiches for lunch. After lunch, they gathered firewood and set up a little area for a campfire. They took selfies in front of the sunset with a beautiful backdrop of the Olympic National Forest behind them. Just before nightfall, they lit the fire, feeling its warmth against the cool evening air. The fire crackled and popped, sending occasional sparks into the twilight. The aroma of burning wood mingled with the fresh scent of pine and earth.

As the light faded, they stoked the campfire, talking about everything and nothing. The savory scent of grilling steaks and chili wafted through the air, making their mouths water.

"This is perfect," Kevin said, flipping the steaks on the grill. "Couldn't ask for a better evening."

Emma smiled, toasting a marshmallow over the fire. "I love it out here. It's so peaceful."

The sizzle of the meat and the bubbling of the chili added to the comforting sounds of the forest night. After dinner, they made the classic s'mores, the sweet aroma of melted chocolate and marshmallows blending with the smoky campfire. They talked a little more, the flickering flames casting dancing shadows on their faces. It got late, close to midnight, so they decided to turn in.

They climbed into the tent, unraveled their sleeping bags, and crawled in, feeling the coolness of the night air against their skin.

"We should do this more often," Emma said, snuggling into her sleeping bag.

"Absolutely," Kevin agreed, as they gave each other a kiss. "Goodnight, babe."

As they drifted off to sleep, the symphony of crickets and distant hoots of an owl filled the night. They weren't quite asleep, halfway between sleep and awake in that neutral state, when Kevin began to feel uneasy.

Stuck in his consciousness and unable to fully wake, he heard footsteps approaching the tent. The dry leaves and gravel on the ground crunched under the weight of the unseen visitor. His restlessness grew, and his anxiety heightened as the footsteps got closer and closer. He felt paralyzed and couldn't move. Then the footsteps were right outside the tent, and whatever it was leaned in from outside the tent. Kevin saw a disembodied human-like apparition, a ghostly figure, looking down at him and Emma, staring straight into his eyes.

With all his strength in his state of slumber, Kevin forced himself awake, startled, screaming, "Get outta here! Get away!"

Emma woke up startled as well, and they both heard something rustle off into the bushes to the right of them and scurry away.

"What the heck was that?" Emma gasped, sitting up.

Kevin panted, trying to catch his breath. "I... I don't know. I thought I was dreaming."

Emma looked at him, her eyes wide. "I had the same exact dream."

"Did you hear that thing go off to the right?" Emma asked.

Kevin replied, "Yes, did you?"

Emma said, "Yes, it was real."

Kevin was stunned. He grabbed the flashlight, opened the tent, and burst out, ready for anything. He shone the light everywhere, but there was nothing. The cold night air bit at them as they looked around.

"I don't see anything," Kevin's voice trembled.

They looked at the area where they heard the footsteps rustle up, and it was almost a sheer wall of a hill and lots of shrubbery and trees, very steep.

"No one could've climbed up there as fast as we heard it leave," Kevin said, perplexed.

"Maybe it was a giant elk," Emma suggested, though she sounded unsure. "But we would've heard more crashing through the bushes, I think."

Startled, Kevin stoked the fire and threw on more wood so it would burn longer and brighter through the night and illuminate the campsite. The comforting crackle of the fire and its warm glow provided a small sense of security. After about an hour of sitting up, things seemed normal. The clear, moonlit sky and stars twinkling above calmed them. The cool night carried the fresh scent of crisp mountain air.

"Let's try gett'n some sleep," Kevin said, his voice soft and uncertain. "We'll figure it out in the morning."

They both decided to turn in again, their minds racing with questions about what they had experienced, but knowing they experienced it together. And then they wondered: Would they be visited again?

Valley of Sorrow

Three couples decided to go camping in the Olympic National Forest: Josh and Shannon, Ken and Courtney, and Darion and Brianna, who brought their two children—a five-year-old boy named Dillan and a ten-year-old girl named Jamie. They ventured deep into a secluded area of the forest, a place not many travelers frequented. The region boasted excellent fishing spots along the creeks and rivers where they chose to camp. It was perfect weather, with beautiful sunshine, fresh mountain air, and large old-growth pine trees adding to the adventure.

As some of the men were fishing, they heard the playful sounds of children at the creek and other distant voices. The flowing river mingled with faint laughter, creating an eerie yet captivating curiosity.

"Do you hear that?" Josh asked, glancing at Ken.

Ken nodded. "Yeah, sounds like kids playing. Could be Jamie and Dillan."

They shrugged it off, thinking perhaps one of their kids was making noise. However, the women also heard strange occurrences around the campground—the crackling of twigs, echoes in the wind, and occasional unexplained laughter.

"Did you hear that?" Shannon whispered to Brianna, her eyes wide.

Brianna nodded. "Yeah, it's strange. But let's not worry about it too much. We're probably just tired."

Despite these oddities, they enjoyed their first evening and spent the night peacefully, lulled to sleep by the gentle hum of the forest.

The next morning, they settled into their routine— cooking breakfast and preparing for the day ahead. The sizzle of bacon and the aroma of freshly brewed coffee filled the air, mixing with the earthy scent of dew-soaked soil. The men went fishing again in the late afternoon, returning to camp for lunch. A park ranger drove up in a forest service van, approached them, and struck up a conversation.

"Good afternoon, folks. I'm Ranger Nox. How's the camping trip so far?" he asked with a friendly smile.

"It's been great, thank you," Darion replied. "We just finished lunch. Are you hungry? We can make you a sandwich."

"No thanks. I ate earlier," Nox replied. "But, if you like, I can give everyone a little tour of the area and share some local legends and historical events if you're interested."

"That sounds great!" Shannon exclaimed. "The kids would love that."

They agreed and climbed into his van, which was big enough to hold everyone, with the worn vinyl seats creaking under their weight.

As they traveled with the ranger, he recounted the area's history, explaining how early English settlers had brutally slaughtered Native Americans, leading to a legend of a curse placed on the land for all eternity. The atmosphere grew heavy with the weight of his words.

"That's a tragic history," Courtney said softly.

Nox nodded. "Indeed. And some say the land is still haunted by those events."

They arrived at a bridge where the ranger stopped and asked everyone to be quiet and listen. They rolled down the windows and, amidst the rustling trees and flowing creek, they faintly heard the sound of people playing in the water. The cool air brushed against their skin, and a chill ran down their spines as the ranger remarked, "Do you hear the voices?"

Everyone agreed in astonishment and disbelief.

"They say that's the sound of the families before they were slaughtered," Nox added.

Everyone glanced at each other, a little spooked.

Continuing their drive, they reached a gate leading to a valley. Shannon got a chill and an uneasy feeling; she warned against entering.

"I don't have a good feeling about this place," Shannon said, her voice trembling. "Let's not go in there. I feel like that's a valley of sorrow," she said with a gasp.

Spooked by the earlier voices, they decided to heed the warning. The ranger acknowledged the valley's tragic history and agreed it was wise not to proceed.

"Eerie things happen in there," Nox said.

They returned to camp and parted ways with the ranger that evening, the sky painted with hues of orange and pink as the sun set.

That night, strange occurrences continued. People began dropping cups and food plates, the clatter echoing in the silence. Dillan, the five-year-old boy, seemingly mesmerized, walked right into the fire.

"Dillan, no!" Brianna screamed, rushing to pull him away from the flames.

The heat from the flames licked at his clothes, but he wasn't seriously hurt, much to everyone's relief. The incident left everyone unsettled, and the cheerful mood of the previous day turned to concern, though they tried to dismiss it as mere ghost stories.

On the third day, curiosity got the better of the men. They decided to explore beyond the gate into the valley, leaving the women and children at the camp.

"Are you sure about this?" Ken asked, glancing at Josh and Darion.

"It will be fun, an adventure. We will be back before noon," Josh replied, determination in his eyes.

They ventured deep into the valley. Time was distorted to them in there; they returned later than they anticipated, early evening, visibly changed. Exhausted from the long hike, their faces were drawn and pale.

"What happened in there?" Shannon asked, worry etched on her face.

"We... we saw things," Darion said, his voice shaking. "Let's just leave it at that."

When it was time to leave, Darion loaded Brianna and their children into their park model camper, with Darion driving and ensuring the safety chains and hitch were secure. The other two couples followed in their vehicles. When they made it to the main road, they gained speed on Highway 101. The engine's hum was abruptly interrupted by a loud bang. They saw sparks flying from the trailer, and the smell of burning metal filled the air. They pulled over to find the trailer hitch had popped off the ball receiver, completely dragging on the road.

"How'd this happen?" Darion exclaimed, inspecting the hitch.

"If it wasn't for the safety chains, the camper would have crashed with Brianna and the kids inside," Josh said, his voice filled with worry.

Rechecking the hitch, Darion was certain it had been properly secured before. Ken added that he had checked it, too, before they left, and confirmed it was secure.

"This time, we'll all ride upfront together," Darion decided.

The family rode in the truck, and they continued home safely.

Life seemed to return to normal, and the couples stayed in touch. However, strange things began to unfold. Josh started to lose his sanity, his once lively eyes becoming hollow and distant. Ken died in a car accident, the screech of tires and shattering glass haunting Courtney's dreams. The most tragic fate befell Darion, who murdered his entire family before taking his own life. Shannon and Courtney were left in shock and grief, their hearts heavy with sorrow.

In their sorrow, the two women questioned why the men had crossed that gate and why the ranger had shown it to them in the first place.

Months had passed since the ill-fated camping trip, yet the haunting memories of the Valley of Sorrow continued to linger in the minds of Shannon and Courtney. The eerie occurrences and tragic events felt like a shadow that refused to lift.

Determined to find answers, the women delved into the history of the area and the legend of the cursed valley. Their search led them to uncover disturbing connections between their experiences and countless others who had ventured into the valley before them. Each story was marked by tragedy.

The realization sent shivers down their spines, the weight of the curse pressed heavily on them.

Sometimes, warning signs come in the form of locked gates, tragic legends, or eerie stories. It may be best to heed them, whether they are posted or not.

Lake Pleasant

It was a beautiful summer day, and the annual fishing derby in the Olympic National Forest was about to get underway. The Beaver Fishing Derby was an all-ages charity fishing event, always held after the first day they stocked Lake Pleasant. This year was special, as they were supposed to stock the lake with extra-large, twenty-four-inch rainbow trout. It had been the talk of the town for weeks leading up to the derby. Everyone had their eye on catching one.

Four friends—Drew and Madi, Kyle and Tiffany—were getting together for a BBQ at the annual summer event. Drew and Madi lived in the trailer park in Beaver, while Kyle and Tiffany drove from Port Angeles to visit their friends. They met up at Drew and Madi's mobile home, jumped into Drew's drop top truck with all the BBQ gear, and headed to the lake. It was only a mile away, so Kyle and Tiff rode in the back.

As the wind whipped through their hair, it made them feel alive.

The group wasn't planning to fish; they were just going to barbecue and enjoy a nice day at the lake's recreational area, which had picnic tables perfect for setting up their propane grill. It was an ideal way to spend a summer day.

On their way out of the park, they saw Gene, the park maintenance supervisor. "How's it going, Gene?" Drew asked. "Just BBQing and having a few beers. Takin' it easy today," Gene replied. "Cool! We're headed to the derby to BBQ," Drew said. "Nice! Stop by afterward if you like. Have a good time." "Who was that?" Kyle asked. "Oh, that's Gene the super. He's a pretty cool guy. He also grows some great ganja," Drew said, as everyone laughed.

Along the way, they stopped at the convenience store to get some ice for the cooler. They got to the park, found a table, and set up the grill. The smell of freshly cut grass filled the air as they each grabbed a cold one from the cooler. "Cheers!" everyone said, raising their drinks in salute. The crisp, refreshing taste of beer was perfect for this warm summer day.

As the day progressed, they enjoyed snacks and a few drinks. They threw a couple of burgers on the grill and a few bean burgers for the girls since they were vegetarians. Drew said, "Got some meat for the men and some bean burgers for the girls. You're lucky I didn't just get you some tofu." In unison, the girls said, "Mmmm!" "I love tofu!" Madi added. "Sheesh," Drew sighed. The sizzle of the burgers on the grill and the savory aroma filled the air, making everyone's mouths water in anticipation.

Suddenly, they saw a man staggering along the lakeshore, drenched from water. Everyone glanced at him but didn't pay much attention to him. He staggered up behind Madi, who had her back turned. Startled, she turned around, and he grabbed her by the shoulders, collapsing on top of her. She screamed as they fell to the ground.

The man's face twisted in agony as he opened his mouth, releasing a torrent of spaghetti-like vomit all over her face. The foul stench hit the group surprisingly fast, like a punch, making everyone gag.

Everyone gasped, almost puking themselves at what they just saw. The sickly, putrid smell of the vomit clung to the air and stuck in their noses like rancid sludge.

She tried to scream and push him off while everyone else yelled in surprise and ran to her aid. Drew shouted at the man to get off, and Kyle kicked him off and away from Madi.

Drew knelt beside her but was afraid to touch her, seeing what was all over her face. Other people in the park also ran up to the scene. Instantly they realized the "spaghetti" was moving. They saw that it was worms. "What the hell!" Drew cried out. He stood up, stumbling backward as the writhing mass came into focus. The slimy, wriggling worms were revolting. The worms crawled into her nose and mouth, choking her as she gasped for air and flailed in panic. They squirmed and wiggled into her body through her face; then she began to convulse like she was having a seizure. Madi began gurgling and spewing things from her mouth, and just as suddenly as it began, it stopped, and she lay still. Then she twitched, rolled over and slowly stood up, just standing there awkwardly with puke and stomach matter still on her face. "Are you okay, honey?" Drew asked. Then she looked at him with searing intent, charged at him, tackled him to the ground, ripped and gnashed at him tearing into his neck as blood spewed everywhere and flesh was torn from his body. Drew gurgled his last few breaths.

At the same time, the man who had been kicked off Madi got up and started staggering toward the onlookers. He grabbed a handful of the worms he had vomited that were on the ground and threw them at the crowd, which stuck to the spectators like cooked spaghetti sticks to a wall. Those who got worms on them panicked, trying to bat them off. The worms took hold of their new hosts, infecting them. Eventually, they fell to the ground and convulsed in seizures. In seconds, they rose as zombie-like creatures looking for prey. They moved clumsily but quickly, capturing and chomping into people, gashing flesh, and causing blood to erupt everywhere. It was a madness no one had ever seen before, except in a horror movie.

The park was a cacophony of screams and shouts, mingling with the grotesque sounds of flesh being torn.

The once serene setting had transformed into a nightmare, with people running in every direction, panic and fear contorting their expressions.

A man in shorts holding a beer stood frozen in shock, watching the terror. A worm landed on his foot and rapidly crawled up his leg. He screamed in fright, shaking his leg and dropping his beer. The worm crawled up his shorts, then he grabbed his butt, screaming, "Get it out! Get it out!" He could feel it slithering as it entered him. He fell down, and began convulsing, after a few seconds he clumsily got up, and then attacked someone trying to run past him, tearing into their flesh and consuming them like BBQ.

Kyle and Tiff witnessed all of this and started panicking. They ran for the truck but realized they didn't have the keys. They sprinted from the park, running about half a mile to the corner store. Their breaths came in ragged gasps, and their hearts pounded in their chests. Bursting inside the store, they asked for a phone and called the sheriff, explaining the chaos. The sheriff, in disbelief, said he'd come down. "This better not be a prank. Someone is getting arrested if it is," he barked and hung up.

As they got off the phone, the clerk and Kyle held the door shut. A man pumping gas fell to the ground, convulsing. Kyle and Tiff said, "He didn't get attacked." "He probably had one of those things on him and didn't know it." The clerk, unsure of what was happening, said,

"He needs help." As he opened the door and ran out to help the man, "No, don't go, come back!" Kyle screamed. But the clerk went anyway, only to be attacked and ripped to shreds by one of the creatures, then two others joining in the buffet.

Then they saw a car driving erratically; it veered off the highway, crashed into a telephone pole, and a person flew out, tumbling onto the ground. The sound of the tires screeching and the car crash rang through the air. Moments later, that person got up, staggering, then started chasing someone who was running. Kyle and Tiff locked the grocery store door. As zombie creatures ran up and began to bang on the glass window, the loud thuds of their fists hitting the glass gave them anxiety and a sense of urgency. They realized they needed to leave.

"Let's get back to the car and get outta here." Kyle muttered and Tiff agreed.

"We should take stuff before we go," Kyle commented with certainty.

"Stuff, like what?" Tiff asked nervously.

"Water and supplies."

They found vehicle emergency roadside backpacks. Kyle's heart pounded as he grabbed them, dumping out the contents to use the backpacks for carrying food and water. We need to be quick. We can't afford to waste any time, he thought. The backpacks were hunter orange but could hold a lot. Their hands shook as they hurriedly packed the supplies.

"I've got water bottles, snacks, and some chili. What else?" Tiff asked with urgency.

"Grab anything that looks useful. We need to be prepared," Kyle replied without hesitation.

They slung the packs over their shoulders and snuck out the back door, running through bushes and trees, kicking up leaves and snapping twigs underfoot until they reached the mobile home park. Their hearts racing while gasping for air.

Surprisingly, Gene was still on his porch, sitting in his lawn chair, grilling, and drinking a beer. "Hey, how you guys doing? Back early, huh?" Gene said, seeing that they were a little disheveled. "Everything okay?"

"No! Everything is crazy!" they shouted, freaking out and asking to come in. They went inside his singlewide mobile home and told Gene everything, recounting the whole gruesome encounter. Gene, skeptical but spooked, locked the door just in case.

They said they were going to get their car that was at Drew's place at the end of the trailer park and get out of there. Gene suggested, "Before we go, we should see the professor who lives just two trailers down. He will probably know what was going on." They agreed, but before they left, Gene locked his place up, grabbed a beer and the BBQ pork rib sandwich he had made before they showed up. Kyle and Tiff gave him a look. "What! I'm hungry. I haven't eaten yet," Gene said.

They ran over to the professor's house and knocked on his door. He answered, and Gene explained a little, asking to come inside. Fearful of standing outside, they went inside, locking the door behind them. The sound of the door lock clicking into place was oddly reassuring. They told the professor what had happened.

The professor, perplexed, said it sounded like a horsehair worm parasite but added that they didn't attack humans. However, if it was a parasite, he might have something that could help. Going through his cupboard, jars clinked together as he searched for the medicine. He found some anti-parasitic medicine left over from his travels in Africa while doing research for his second doctoral thesis. "Don't take those yet. We need to find out what's going on," the professor said with a concerned look on his face.

Just then, they heard screams and looked out the window, seeing people being attacked. The chaos had spread to the park. It seemed to be everywhere. The screams and sounds of struggle echoed through the park. They turned on the news and realized the infection had spread. The news advised everyone to stay indoors, secure and lock doors and windows, avoid contact with people, especially the infected, and have enough provisions for 3 to 7 days. "This should be resolved soon. In the meantime, stay inside," the newscaster said.

Gene's face paled as he listened to the news. "This can't be real. How could this happen?" he grumbled, shaking his head in disbelief.

Tiffany clung to Kyle, her eyes wide with fear. "What's happening, Kyle? What do we do?" she whispered, her voice trembling.

They decided to reinforce the doors and windows. "What about food and water?" Gene asked. "We got some food and water from the grocery store," Kyle said. They began filling jugs and empty containers with water. The sound of water pouring into the containers was unexpectedly calming. They filled the tub full of water and put a shower curtain over it to minimize evaporation and debris. "How'd you know to do that?" Tiff asked. "My uncle used to have a pool when I was a kid. He taught me a few things. I figured this would work too," Kyle replied. "Better to collect and save this water now in case it gets shut off."

The professor, uneasy about everything, decided to call a colleague for more answers. His hands trembled as he dialed his colleague's number. "Please, let there be an answer," he whispered, his heart heavy with dread.

His colleague answered the phone, they greeted each other, and the professor asked if he knew what was going on. His colleague said there was an infection that was widespread, turning people into zombies across the U.S. It wasn't just Lake Pleasant or Seattle; it was everywhere. The infection was spreading through cities, states, and beyond.

During the phone conversation, the professor learned that this was an attack from an unfriendly country, possibly a preemptive attack that had gotten out of hand. High-altitude balloons had dropped payloads of genetically modified zombie-infecting worms across the United States. The worms had spread undetected, through their initial incubation period, then all at once escalated into a major crisis.

He learned these horsehair worms entered the body and attached to the nervous system or brainstem, taking over the host completely. Infected individuals became ravenous and attacked non-infected people, eating them, fueling what was going to happen next. Those who got bitten or were exposed to blood or saliva from an infected person usually became infected with microscopic worms. The transition for these victim hosts was slower, but they would eventually turn.

After the host was taken over and had become a complete zombie, another incubation period began. The worms would multiply rapidly, reaching thousands inside the body, growing into full-grown adults. These new adult parasites were then ejected onto new hosts through violent vomiting or diarrhea. "Oh jeez!" the professor exclaimed, after hearing the details.

The only treatment found to slow the infection was anti-parasitic pills like albendazole and ivermectin. These provided some resistance but were not known to fully prevent infection. The colleague continued and said that infected individuals remained extremely violent, dangerous, and most of all contagious.

After a brief pause, the voice on the phone said, "Wade, this thing is out of control. There are reports that this is happening all over the world. We don't have a solution or a cure yet." He went on to say that if communications went down, he would post updates on the Satellite Mesh network. "Good luck," he added, and then he hung up the phone.

Realizing the gravity of the situation, everyone looked at each other in disbelief and horror. "We need to protect ourselves; we need to get weapons," Kyle said.

Epilogue:

They gathered some weapons. Gene snuck out the back door and returned with extra food and a shotgun with a box of shells from his trailer. "It's not much, but it'll have to do. No use in staying at my place; it's better here."

The professor nodded. "I have a flare gun in case we need to signal for help."

They continued reinforcing the professor's doublewide, doing their best to block all entry points. Outside, the chaos continued to spread. Infected people—no, zombies—were everywhere, turning the once peaceful community into a living nightmare.

Inside, they stayed vigilant and quiet, taking turns keeping watch. The atmosphere was tense, with every noise outside raising alarm. They knew they had to survive and hoped for the authorities to bring the situation under control.

Days passed, each one filled with anxiety and fear. The news reports became sporadic as the infection spread, but they held on to hope. The anti-parasitic medicine seemed to work for now, but they knew it was a race against time. Survival was no longer a choice; it was their only option. In the end, resilience and determination were their greatest weapons.

Dear Reader,

I hope you enjoyed these stories as much as I enjoyed creating them. I hope they added a little excitement to your campfire gatherings with friends and family, and that you got a little spooked by the tales. Thank you for all your encouragement and support.

Warmest Regards,

R.S. Hughes

www.ingramcontent.com/pod-product-compliance
Lightning Source LLC
Chambersburg PA
CBHW070802120626
46557CB00002B/683